Fuzzypeg Goes to School

Alison Uttley
pictures by Margaret Tempest

COLLINS

William Collins Sons & Co Ltd
London · Glasgow · Sydney · Auckland
Toronto · Johannesburg

First published 1938
© text The Alison Uttley Literary Property Trust 1986
© illustrations The Estate of Margaret Tempest 1986
© this arrangement William Collins Sons & Co Ltd 1990

Cover decoration by Fiona Owen
Decorated capital by Mary Cooper
Alison Uttley's original story has been abridged for this book.
A CIP catalogue record for this book is
available from the British Library.

ISBN 0-00-193124-5

Made and printed in Great Britain by
BPCC Paulton Books Limited.

FOREWORD

Of course you must understand that Grey Rabbit's home had no electric light or gas, and even the candles were made from pith of rushes dipped in wax from the wild bees' nests, which Squirrel found. Water there was in plenty, but it did not come from a tap. It flowed from a spring outside, which rose up from the ground and went to a brook. Grey Rabbit cooked on a fire, but it was a wood fire, there was no coal in that part of the country. Tea did not come from India, but from a little herb known very well to country people, who once dried it and used it in their cottage homes. Bread was baked from wheat ears, ground fine, and Hare and Grey Rabbit gleaned in the cornfields to get the wheat.

The doormats were plaited rushes, like country-made mats, and cushions were stuffed with wool gathered from the hedges where sheep pushed through the thorns. As for the looking-glass, Grey Rabbit found the glass, dropped from a lady's handbag, and Mole made a frame for it. Usually the animals gazed at themselves in the still pools as so many country children have done. The country ways of Grey Rabbit were the country ways known to the author.

 t was bedtime, and little Fuzzypeg the Hedgehog sat by the fire in his night-gown eating his bread and milk. His mother was mending his blue smock which he had torn on his prickles.

"Will my father tell me a tale tonight?" asked Fuzzypeg.

"If you're a good hedgehog and eat every bit of your supper," said Mrs Hedgehog kindly.
Old Hedgehog hung up his milking yoke and came into the cosy room.

"Please tell me a bedtime story," implored Fuzzypeg.

Old Hedgehog rubbed his hands and scratched his head, trying to think of a nice tale.

Then he began to sing,

"A Frog he would a-wooing go,
Whether his mother would let him or no,
Heigh! Ho! says Rowley."

Fuzzypeg beat time with the spoon on the wooden bowl, and Mrs Hedgehog forgot to thread her needle as she listened.

"What a lovely tale!" cried Fuzzypeg.

"I larned that in my schooldays, when I was a youngster, same as Fuzzypeg," said Hedgehog, modestly.

"Can I go to school and learn poems?" asked Fuzzypeg

"I think he's big enough, don't you, Hedgehog?" And Mrs Hedgehog looked at her husband.

"Yes. It's about time he had some eddication," replied Hedgehog. "You can't get on without wisdom. Just think what a lot Wise Owl knows."

"Can I go to school tomorrow?" Fuzzypeg asked, jumping down from his stool.

"Yes, if I've mended these holes in time," Mrs Hedgehog told him. Fuzzypeg hopped round the room for joy. Then he went to say goodnight to the world.

"Goodnight Star," he called to the evening star, and it nodded goodnight, and hid behind a cloud, for it was shocked that Fuzzypeg wasn't asleep.

The next morning he awoke early and sprang out of bed in a great hurry.

"I'm going to school today," he sang, as he rolled downstairs in a prickly ball.

Old Hedgehog had been out since dawn, milking the cows and carrying milk to his customers.

Fuzzypeg saw him returning and ran to meet him. The hedgehog carried something under his arm and Fuzzypeg danced round, asking what it was.

"Wait a minute. Don't be in such a hurry," said Old Hedgehog.

He gave Mrs Hedgehog the milk for breakfast, then he sat down and slowly opened the parcel. Then he took from the leafy paper a little leather bag. Fuzzypeg turned it over with cries of excitement.

"A school bag! A school bag! Look Mother! Where has it come from?"

Fuzzypeg showed his mother all the pockets. There was a big one for sandwiches, two little ones for lesson books and a tiny one for the penny to pay for the schooling.

"Grey Rabbit gave it to me when she heard you were going to school," said Hedgehog. "I took the milk as usual this morning, and I tells her, 'My Fuzzypeg's going to get Wisdom same as Wise Owl.' 'Indeed,' sez she. 'Wait a minute, Hedgehog.' So I stood on the doorstep, and then Grey Rabbit comes downstairs, carrying this.

" 'A lesson bag for Fuzzypeg,' sez she."

"What shall I put in it?" asked Fuzzypeg, turning it inside out.

"Your lessons – sums and poems and tales," said Hedgehog, "and your sandwiches for elevenses, and your penny for the schoolmaster."

Then they all had a good breakfast, and Fuzzypeg started off for school with the leather bag on his back.

"Don't talk too much, and don't be late," said his mother, as she waved good-bye.

As he went down the lane he saw his cousins, Tim and Bill Hedgehog, who lived in the cottage in the larch wood.

"Hello, Fuzzypeg!" they called. "Where are you going with that fine bag?"

"I'm going to school," said Fuzzypeg.

"Wait a minute. We'll come too," they cried and ran to their mother. "Mother! Mother! Can we go to school with Fuzzypeg?"

"Yes. If Fuzzypeg is big enough, so are you," said their mother.

She brushed their quills and cut their sandwiches, and sent them off.

"I say, do be quick," called Fuzzypeg. "We shall be late."

"Late? What's late?" asked Tim.

"I don't know. Something we musn't be," replied Fuzzypeg.

They trotted along the lane, when whom should they see but Hare, lolloping along in his bright blue coat.

"Hello, Fuzzypeg! Hello young'uns!" he called. "Have you seen my shadow? It's not anywhere about. I don't know where I put it."

"Perhaps it's in Robin Postman's nest," suggested Fuzzypeg, and he knocked at the door of a neat nest in the bank.

"Yes, what is the matter?" asked Robin Postman, popping out his head.

"Have you seen Hare's shadow anywhere about?" asked Fuzzypeg.

"No. Has he lost it?" The little postman looked up at the sky.

"Of course he hasn't a shadow!" Robin exclaimed. "None of you has a shadow."

The three hedgehogs looked all around them.

"No, we haven't. Oh dear! We can't go to school without shadows!" they cried.

"Wait till the sun comes out, then your shadows will leap back to you," advised Robin, going inside and shutting his door.

"What is inside your bag, Fuzzypeg?" asked Hare.

"Sandwiches," said Fuzzypeg, and he brought them out and divided them.

"Now you have room for other things," said Hare, and they gathered bindweed, forget-me-nots and foxgloves.

"Now," continued Hare, "if you'll sit down on this bank I will teach you. First, where is your money?"

Fuzzypeg took his bright penny from his bag and gave it to Hare.

"I'll teach you your ABC," said Hare.

"A. Hay grows in the Daisy Field, when the sun shines," he said.

"I like Hay," said Fuzzypeg.

"B. Bees live in gardens. They get honey and that is a good thing."

"I've been stung by a bee," said Tim Hedgehog.

"C. Seas are very wet. They are all water and they never dry up," said Hare.

"I shouldn't like to fall in C," said Fuzzypeg, and the others agreed.

"That's all for today. You know your ABC," said Hare, suddenly running off, for he had spied little Grey Rabbit coming towards them.

Little Grey Rabbit came along the path with her basket on her arm. When she saw the three little hedgehogs sitting on the grass, she was astonished.

"What are you doing here, Fuzzypeg?" she asked. "I thought you were at school."

"We are waiting for the sun to come out. We can't go to school without our shadows."

"Of course you can! Now run along as fast as you can, or your teacher will be very cross."

So off they ran, under the gate to the Daisy Field, and across the meadow to the little pasture where Jonathan Rabbit had his school.

A sweet little tinkle came from the pasture.

"There's the school bell," said a thrush. "You'll be late. Young Hare always rings the hare-bells you know. He's been jingling them for a long time now."

So they ran, puffing and panting towards the sound of the blue bells.

"I've got a stitch in my side," groaned Bill, and he drank from a stream to cure his pain.

"I've cut my leg on a bramble," cried Tim, and he stopped to find a cobweb to bind up the wound.

"I've tored my smock on the gorse-bush," said Fuzzypeg, and he looked for a thorn to pin it together.

In the distance little Hare stood in a grove of slender hare-bells, shaking the bells for the last time. Then he ran into school, and there was silence.

Then the three hedgehogs raced across the pasture to the school door.

They knocked at a little green door with a brass knocker hidden in low bushes.

They entered a room whose walls were made of closely-woven blackberry bushes. The ceiling of the schoolroom was the blue sky, where the sun was now shining, so that the little hedgehogs saw their shadows as they walked shyly across the room to old Jonathan.

"Benjamin Hedgehog.

"Timothy Hedgehog.

"Fuzzypeg Hedgehog," said he, writing
their names on a rose leaf. "Each of you is

'A diller, a dollar

A ten-o'clock scholar.'
Remember that school begins at nine o'clock, and
don't be late."

They sat down by the side of the hedgehogs, squirrels,
rabbits, the young hare, a small mole and some field
mice. They all read from books made of green leaves
which Jonathan gave them.

Then he asked them some questions, and all the
little animals stood up in a row, with Fuzzypeg at
the end.

"Which flower helps a rabbit to remember?" he asked.

Fuzzypeg drew the blue forget-me-nots from his lesson bag and held them up.

"Quite right, Fuzzypeg. Go to the top of the class," said Jonathan.

"Which flower shuts its eyes when it rains?" he asked.

Fuzzypeg held up the white trumpet of the climbing bindweed.

Then Jonathan asked his last question.

"Which flower makes gloves for cold paws?"

Every animal knew the answer, and they all shouted, "Foxgloves," before Fuzzypeg could get the purple foxglove from his satchel.

"Now for a counting lesson," said Jonathan.

"One, two, buckle my shoe," sang the animals, and all the little hedgehogs fastened their shoes.

"Three, four, knock at the door," they sang.

"Five, six, pick up sticks," and they ran into the pasture to gather as many sticks as they could carry.

"Seven, eight, lay them straight," and each tried to lay his sticks in even lengths.

"Eleven o'clock," said Jonathan, blowing at a dandelion clock. "Go and eat your sandwiches."

Suddenly Fuzzypeg saw a little figure in a grey dress coming across the Daisy Field, towards the school.

"Here's little Grey Rabbit!" he called and all the animals rushed to meet her, and begged her to sit down and tell them a story.

She sat on a tuffet in the shade of a hawthorn-tree, and began the tale of Red Riding Hood. She had just got to the part where Red Riding Hood came to her grand-mother's cottage, when there was a mighty roaring noise close by, from behind the hawthorn-tree.

"Woof! Woof! Woof! I'll nab you!" came a terrible voice.

"Oh! Oh!" they all shrieked. "Oh! the Wolf!" And they all ran helter-skelter up and down the field.

Grey Rabbit stood very still, for she thought she recognised the voice, though it was different in some way.

"Boo! Boo! Woof! Woof! I'll nab you," roared the creature, gruffly.

"Come out Hare," said Grey Rabbit sternly. "Come out at once. You can't deceive *me*."

From behind the tree came Hare, holding a cone-shaped trumpet, made from the bark of a silver-birch tree.

"Ha! Ha! I frightened you. You thought it was a Wolf, didn't you?"

All the little animals came creeping out to stare at the trumpet that Hare carried; all, except Fuzzypeg.

"Where's Fuzzypeg?" asked little Grey Rabbit.

"Where's Fuzzypeg?" echoed the others.

Then they heard a squeaky little voice.

"A-tishoo!" it said. "Help! A-tishoo! A-tishoo!"

From out of the stream crawled a very bedraggled little hedgehog.

"C is very wet," he said. "A-tishoo!"

"Poor little Fuzzypeg," said Grey Rabbit, running up to him. "You'd better go straight home to bed."

"School, DISMISS!" shouted Jonathan.

"A holiday. No more school today."

All the little animals leaped up and down crying:
"A holiday!"

"I didn't want a holiday. I've only just begun," said
Fuzzypeg in a quavering voice. "A-tishoo!"

But Grey Rabbit took him by the hand, and hurried
him home, while Hare ran alongside.

"Whatever have you been and gone and done?"
asked Mrs Hedgehog, holding up her hands in horror
when she saw her wet little son.

Little Grey Rabbit explained what had happened, and Hare said, "I'm very sorry, Mrs Hedgehog. It shan't occur again." Then he ran away, leaping home.

"You must put Fuzzypeg to bed at once, Mrs Hedgehog," said Grey Rabbit.

So little Fuzzypeg was popped into his warm bed, with a bowl of delicious gruel and black-currant tea.

Grey Rabbit sat at his bedside and she sang little songs to him while Fuzzypeg sneezed and sneezed again.

When little Grey Rabbit started for home, Fuzzypeg croaked "Good-bye, Grey Rabbit." And then he shut his eyes and slept till his father came home.

"What did they larn you besides swimming, my son?" asked Old Hedgehog, as he looked at little Fuzzypeg.

"Hay, Bee and Sea. I think that was what Hare taught us. I fell into C, Father, And tomorrow we're going to learn 'Here we go gathering nuts in May.' I like school, Father."

"You've not larned much," said Old Hedgehog, "and they say, 'A little larning is a dangerous thing.' You'd better get a bit more knowledge tomorrow, and don't go to Mr Hare for your lessons neither."